Game Time, Mallory!

To Amy Fitzgerald, an incredible editor!
Thanks for keeping Mallory in the game.
—L.B.F.

For Jinx, our sweet dog from 4 Paws for Ability, and for
Elliot, Max, Makayla, Carter, Alex, Grace, Ben, Anthony,
Alec, Abbie, Nelson, Finn, Noah & Madison, whose amazing
families are on this journey with us. You will have a
special place in my heart, always.
—J.K.

by Laurie Friedman
illustrations by Jennifer Kalis

MINNEAPOLIS

CONTENTS

A WORD FROM MALLORY

My name is Mallory McDonald, like the restaurant, but no relation. I'm in fourth grade. I have a cat named Cheeseburger and a brother named Max, and my best friends—Mary Ann, Joey, and Chloe Jennifer—all live on my street. It's called Wish Pond Road, and it has a real wish pond on it that I can go to whenever I need to make a wish.

All that's great, but today, things got even better because of a letter that came in the mail. It said there's a new basketball league in Fern Falls for fourth- and fifth-grade girls. All you have to do to play in the league is try out, and then you get placed on a team.

Joey plays on a soccer team, and Max has played on a baseball team for as long as I can remember. I've never been on a sports team, and I knew this could be my chance.

"Max, you've always loved being on a team. Now I'm going to be on one too! It's going to be so, so, so much fun!" I got so excited just picturing myself playing basketball and having a great time with my friends that I started jumping up and down in the kitchen.

It made Mom laugh, but not my brother. "Being on a team isn't all fun and games," said Max. He shook his head just like he always does when he thinks I'm being dumb.

But I don't care what Max thinks! The only two people's opinions I care about are Mary Ann's and Chloe Jennifer's. I bet they're going to be just as excited about playing basketball as I am, and I can't wait to talk to them! I hope they'll have just one thing to say.

It's the same thing I'm saying, which is— SIGN ME UP!

COUNT ME IN

"What do you mean you don't want to sign up?" I say.

I stick my head inside Mary Ann's bedroom window. We always use the window when we have something extra important to say to each other. But Mary Ann looks like she thinks what we're talking about isn't extra important at all.

"Mallory, I have a hip-hop show at the end of the month. I don't have time to play basketball. And to be honest, it doesn't sound like much fun to me anyway."

I try not to pass out when she says that. I don't want to be known as the girl from Wish Pond Road who fainted outside her best friend's window. But I just don't get how Mary Ann thinks playing in this league won't be fun.

Mary Ann and I have always done things together—painting our toenails the same color, chewing the same kind of gum, and even saying things three times. Now we have a chance to do something really fun and new together, and I want to convince her we should do it.

I fish the letter out of my back pocket and hold it out in front of her. "Of course it will be fun. We'll get to meet girls from other schools. We'll have our own uniforms. People will come to cheer for us. It'll be exciting!"

Mary Ann shakes her head like that isn't enough to sell her on the idea, so I keep going.

"Besides, since this is the first time most girls will be playing basketball, there are only five games in the regular season plus the playoffs. It won't take up that much time. You'll still be able to do hip-hop."

Mary Ann rolls her eyes like that's not a good reason either. "Mallory, the games are on Saturday, which means we wouldn't be able to watch *Fashion Fran* when it comes on."

I can't believe Mary Ann thinks watching a TV show, even though it is our favorite one, is more important than playing basketball.

"C'mon!" I say. "It's only for a few weeks."

"Why do you want to do this so badly?" Mary Ann asks. "You don't even know how to play basketball."

I blow a piece of hair off my face. "That's the whole point," I say. "I want to *learn* how to play. I want to try something new. And you should too!"

Mary Ann snort-laughs, which I know means she thinks the idea of learning to play basketball is silly. "Sorry, Mallory," she says. But I can't tell if she's sorry or not.

"I'm going to talk to Chloe Jennifer," I say. Maybe Mary Ann doesn't want to play, but I have my toes crossed that Chloe Jennifer will.

I can hear Mary Ann closing her window as I walk off. She's my best friend, but sometimes, she can be so frustrating.

I walk to Chloe Jennifer's house and ring her doorbell. "Did you get the letter about the new basketball league?" I ask when she opens the door.

Chloe Jennifer nods. "I got it."

"Great! So you're going to play." I knew Chloe Jennifer would want to. "Let's start practicing right away so we're ready for tryouts!" I say.

But Chloe Jennifer shakes her head. "Mallory, I can't play in the basketball league. I have dance lessons every Wednesday and Saturday and a big recital at the end of the school year. Plus, I have piano lessons on Tuesdays. I don't have time to play basketball."

I put my hand on my hip. This is NOT what I expected to happen!

"Mary Ann doesn't want to play either," I tell Chloe Jennifer. Then I give her my best *basketball-would-be-a-whole-lot-more-fun-if-my-best-friends-were-playing-it-with-me* look. "Don't you think it will be fun to be part of a team?"

"I'm sure it would be," says Chloe

Jennifer. Then she pauses like she feels bad and is trying to think of just the right thing to say. "I'm sorry, Mallory. I can't play, but I'm sure a lot of our other friends will want to."

The good news is that Chloe Jennifer is right. When I get to my classroom the next morning, it's what everyone is talking about.

"I'm playing," says April.

"Me too," says Zoe.

"Me three," adds Grace.

"I'm in," says Danielle.

"So am I," says Arielle. "And so is my big sister, Olivia. She played in another league for a year, and she's awesome. She's going to teach Danielle and me everything she knows."

April, Zoe, Grace, and I look at each other as Arielle and Danielle high-five each other.

Zoe rolls her eyes at me.

I know she's thinking what I'm thinking—
which is that Arielle and Danielle can be so
obnoxious and that basketball would be a
whole lot more fun if they weren't playing.
But I don't care. Basketball will still be lots
of fun.

The only thing that would make it more
fun is if Mary Ann and Chloe Jennifer were
playing too. I'm just glad some of the other
girls in my class will be.

When I get home from school, Mom asks
if I want a snack.

"No time for that," I say. I go in Max's
closet to look for his basketball. I need to
start practicing for tryouts.

"Hey! What do you think you're doing?"
Max asks when he sees me in his room.

"Basketball tryouts are next week," I tell
my brother. "I want to be in tip-top shape."

I come out of his closet with his basketball in my hand. I toss it up and catch it. "Want to shoot some hoops with me?" Max rolls his eyes and shakes his head like I just asked him to do something really crazy, like jump off a tall building.

But I don't have time to worry about who is or isn't playing basketball with me. I, Mallory McDonald, have some hoops to shoot!

READY, SET, SHOOT!

When I get to the gym, I squeeze into a seat on the bleachers with April, Zoe, and Grace. I look around the Fern Falls High School gym, which is filled up with fourth and fifth graders who are trying out for the league. There are lots of girls I know from my school, but there are two other elementary schools in Fern Falls, so there are lots of girls I don't know.

I watch as Arielle and Danielle sit down in the row behind us. Arielle leans forward. "Are you guys nervous?" she asks.

"I'm so nervous," I say. Even though I've been practicing on the basketball hoop in my driveway every day for a week, I'm still not sure I'm ready.

"I'm nervous too!" says April.

Zoe nods her head like we can add her name to the nervous list.

"I could hardly sleep last night," says Grace.

Arielle grins like she's not scared at all. "I'm ready," she says.

"So am I," adds Danielle.

"They *would* say that," April mumbles to me.

I make an *I-totally-agree* face. The truth is that they might be saying it, but I don't think they mean it. As I look around the packed gym, I don't see how they couldn't be nervous about trying out in front of so many people.

"Some of the girls are really tall," says Zoe.

"I was thinking the same thing," says Grace.

When a whistle blows, the gym gets quiet.

"Girls, may I have your attention, please." A woman in a blue sweat suit with the initials *FFGBL* on it and a whistle around her neck walks to the center of the floor. There's a lineup of six men and women standing behind her, all wearing the same sweat suit she's wearing. "I'm Coach Nelson, founder and director of the new Fern Falls Girls Basketball League. Welcome, everyone."

The gym fills with clapping and a few whistles.

Coach Nelson nods like she appreciates the enthusiasm. "There will be six teams in the league. During tryouts, all of you will be evaluated based on your ability and placed on a team."

She pauses and looks down at a clipboard she's holding, and then she keeps talking.

"There will be one week of preseason practice, then five games during the regular season, with each team playing all the other teams once. When the regular season ends, the top four teams will go to the playoffs and the two winning teams will advance to the finals. The winning team will be the league champion."

There's another round of clapping and cheering. Coach Nelson waits until the clapping dies down. Then she points to the other men and women wearing FFGBL sweat suits. "I would now like to introduce your coaches."

She turns and faces the lineup of coaches. "Coaches, please wave as I call your names and team names."

All the coaches grin like they're excited to get started. I watch as Coach Nelson introduces the coaches for the Fever, the Liberty, the Storm, the Mystics, the Sparks, and the Dream.

When she's done, Coach Nelson explains how tryouts will work. "When your name is called, you will come to the floor and take three shots. You will start by attempting a three-point shot, then move up to the free throw line and shoot a free throw, and then you will run toward the basket and go for a layup. When you have taken all three shots, you will run and dribble the ball to the other basket and shoot a layup there as well."

Coach Nelson pauses. "Girls, you have four chances to show us what you're made of. Good luck, and let's get ready to play some basketball!"

The gym fills with whistles and claps again. It's easy to see that lots of girls are excited about tryouts.

Coach Nelson calls out the first girl, Catherine Abbott. I watch as she shoots her first three shots, then dribbles across the court to make her fourth shot. Catherine makes two out of four shots. "Not bad," April whispers in my ear.

I nod. I'd be happy to make two out of my four shots.

"Do you think they're going in alphabetical order?" asks Zoe. But before I can answer, we hear Coach Nelson say "Zoe Anderson," into the microphone.

"They must be," says Grace.

"Good luck!" I say to Zoe. Usually I don't like having to wait until my name is called, but today I don't mind that *McDonald* is in the middle of the list. April, Grace, and I squeeze hands as Zoe shoots. She makes two of her four shots, just like the girl before her.

We all high-five Zoe when she walks back over to us. Then we settle in on the bleachers and watch as Coach Nelson calls up girls whose last names begin with B, C, D, and E. Lots of girls make one and two points. Only one girl doesn't make any points, and two girls make three points.

Coach Nelson calls out Arielle Fine when she gets to F.

"Go, Arielle!" Danielle screams from behind where April, Zoe, Grace, and I are sitting.

I watch as Arielle makes one, then two, and then three shots. She misses her last shot, but she looks happy.

"Good job!" Danielle says when she sits down.

Her older sister, Olivia, pats her on the shoulder. "Way to go, Sis!" As Olivia walks to the floor to take her turn, I can't help but think how nice she was to her little sister, who is just starting to play basketball. I wish I could say the same thing about Max.

We all watch from the bleachers as Olivia shoots and makes all four baskets.

"She's awesome," Zoe whispers in my ear. I nod. Arielle and Danielle both high-five her as she walks back to her seat.

Coach Nelson continues calling girls in alphabetical order. Zoe, Grace, and I scream and clap like crazy when she calls out "April Johnson." We watch as April shoots. She makes a free throw and her second layup.

"Great job!" I say as she sits down.

Zoe hugs April. "We both made two shots!"

I try to swallow, but I feel like there's
a basketball stuck in my throat. I know
my turn is coming up soon, and I hope I
do as well as my friends did. The closer
Coach Nelson gets to the letter *M*, the
more nervous I get. When she calls Natalia
Lopez, I feel myself starting to sweat, even
though I haven't started playing yet. I know
I should be watching Natalia shoot, but I
close my eyes, pretend like I'm at the wish

pond on my street, and make a wish.

I wish I will make at least two baskets, just like my friends.

When Coach Nelson calls my name, I can hardly feel my legs as I walk to the three-point line. I tell myself to stay calm. I made lots of baskets when I practiced in my driveway.

"Go, Mallory!" I hear my friends yell.

Coach Nelson blows her whistle. That's my cue to start shooting.

I shoot my three-point shot and miss. I still have three shots that I can make. I go to the free throw line and take the ball one of the coach's hands to me.

I aim. I shoot. I miss!

"C'mon, Mallory!" I hear April yell.

I know this is not a good time to be nervous. I still have two chances to make baskets, and that's what I'm going to do.

C'mon, Mallory. I dribble toward the basket for my layup—and miss again! I can't believe I missed my third shot. I have to make my last one. I don't even stop to think. I dribble it across the court and shoot. I watch as the ball circles the rim. *Go in!* I silently beg it to go through the hoop, but it rolls off the rim and hits the ground.

I try not to groan. Coach Nelson thanks me as I walk to my seat.

"Don't worry," says April when I sit down.

"You were so close on that last shot," says Zoe.

"Close doesn't count," Arielle says from behind me.

Zoe turns around and gives Arielle a *you-should-know-when-to-shut-your-mouth* look. That is clearly something Arielle doesn't know. But the truth is that she's right. I can't believe I missed all four shots.

When Coach Nelson calls "Grace Reyes" and then "Danielle Rose," I watch as they shoot. Both of them only make one basket, but still, they each made one more than I did.

That's what I'm still thinking about as the last girl who is trying out takes her turn. Even though there are several girls who didn't make any of their shots, I don't like that I'm one of them.

"Thanks to you all for coming out today," says Coach Nelson. "You will be getting phone calls on Tuesday night from your coaches to welcome you to the team you're on and give you details for your practice schedules. Good luck! I hope it's a great season for all."

I hope it will be a great season too, and it'll be especially great for me if I'm on a team with at least one of my friends. It would be so much fun to play with Zoe or April or Grace. I cross my toes inside my sneakers and make my second wish of the day.

I wish I'll be on a team with at least one of my friends.

I sure hope this wish comes true.

TEAMMATES

"Mallory, telephone!"

I run to the kitchen when Mom calls me. I take the phone from her. I'm hoping this will be my new coach calling to tell me what team I'm on. I cross my toes that he'll also be telling me that at least one of my friends is on it with me.

"Hi, Mallory," a man's voice says into the phone when I answer. "I'm Coach Darren from Fern Falls Girls Basketball, and I'm

calling to let you
know you're on my
team, the Dream."

Coach Darren
sounds serious
but nice. "Great!"
I say like I'm
excited to be on
the Dream. And I
am. Sort of. I'm glad

to know who my coach is and what team
I'm on. Now I just want to know who is on it
with me.

Coach Darren must be a mind reader
because before I can ask, he tells me.
"Mallory, there are eight girls on the team—
four fourth graders and four fifth graders."
Then he reads off the list of names.

"The fourth graders are you, Arielle
Fine, Danielle Rose, and Liz Chen. The fifth

graders are Olivia Fine, Bree Williams, Daisy Sanchez, and Amanda Moore."

When he's done reading the list, I can feel my shoulders slump. April's not on my team and neither are Grace or Zoe. But Danielle AND Arielle are both on it, and so is Arielle's older sister, Olivia.

Arielle and Danielle can be so mean. It wasn't nice at tryouts when they said they weren't nervous after April, Grace, Zoe, and I all said we were. And it *really* wasn't nice when I didn't make any baskets and Arielle said, "Close doesn't count."

Plus, that wasn't the first time they've been mean. When we performed together in the show *Annie*, they pretended to be my friends and then tried to come between Mary Ann and me. It caused a big problem. Just thinking about it makes me as upset as I was when it happened.

But I don't have much time to think about what happened, because Coach Darren is still talking. "Our first practice will be this weekend," he says. "I'll e-mail you and your parents the details about where and when. Get lots of sleep this week so you're ready to play."

"I will. Thanks, Coach," I say. I don't want Coach Darren to think I have a problem with who is or is not on my team.

When I hang up, Mom asks me about the call.

I know that if I tell her I'm not happy I'm on the same team with Arielle and Danielle, she'll just say that there are five other girls on the team too and that I should make the best of it.

So all I tell Mom is that I'm on the Dream and that we'll be getting details about the practices soon. Then I say that I have some phone calls to make. "I want to talk to my friends and see what team they're on."

Mom smiles like she's glad to see I'm enthusiastic about basketball. But I'm not sure enthusiastic is what I'm feeling right now. I wish my friends were on my team, but what I really wish is that I wasn't on the same team with Danielle AND Arielle.

I take a deep breath and try to calm myself down as I dial Zoe's number.

As soon as Zoe picks up, she starts telling me all about her team. "Mallory, I was just about to call you! I'm on the Mystics. My coach says we're going to have a great season. She sounds really nice, and I think playing basketball will be amazing! Plus, Grace is on my team."

"That's great," I say. And it is great for Zoe and Grace. I just wish I was on their team too.

"So what team are you on?" Zoe asks.

She listens as I tell her about being on the same team with Arielle and Danielle—and Arielle's sister, Olivia.

"Well, Olivia seems like a great player. It might be OK," Zoe says.

I'm thinking the same thing.

I call April next. She tells me about her team, the Storm.

"I wish we were on the same team," I say when she's done talking. Then I tell her about the Dream and that I'm playing with Arielle and Danielle.

"Once the season starts, I don't think it will matter who is on your team," says April.

I really hope she's right. I think about it as I go to bed, and it's what's on my mind the next morning as I walk to school with Mary Ann and Chloe Jennifer.

"Yuck!" says Mary Ann when I tell her about my team. She sticks out her tongue and clutches her stomach. She knows how mean Arielle and Danielle can be.

"I just don't get how they got to be on the same team—and Arielle's older sister too," I say.

Mary Ann makes a *hmmm* sound like she's thinking about it. "I bet their moms requested that they be put together so they could carpool or something."

"That's probably what happened," I say.

Chloe Jennifer links an arm through mine. "Don't focus on them," she says. "You were so excited to learn to play basketball and be on a team. Don't let Arielle and Danielle ruin it for you."

I think about this. It's good advice. "That's what I'm going to do," I say. I smile. Knowing I can talk to my friends makes me feel better, but my smile disappears as soon as I walk into my classroom.

Arielle and Danielle are standing by the door, almost like they're waiting for me. "Mallory, you're on our team," says Arielle like it's *her* team.

"Tell her what your dad said," adds Danielle.

Arielle nods like she's happy to be the one with important news. "My dad has met Coach Darren. He says Coach Darren played basketball in college and is the league's best coach. He also said Coach Darren told him that my sister, Olivia, is one of the top players in the league and that we have a great team. He has high hopes that we'll be the league champions."

"That's great!" I say.

Arielle and Danielle give each other a *who's-going-to-talk-next?* look.

Danielle starts. "Mallory, you didn't make any baskets at tryouts."

Arielle takes it from there. "We just hope you're going to practice at home before our team practices start next week. We want to be sure everyone on our team is in great shape."

"You get what we mean?" Danielle asks me.

I nod. "I'll be ready," I tell them. Then I think about what Chloe Jennifer said. I'm going to try not to let Arielle and Danielle ruin basketball for me.

But as the saying goes . . . that's going to be easier said than done.

PRACTICE IMPERFECT

"Mallory, let's go!" Mom yells. "You'll be late!"

I rub the fur behind Cheeseburger's ears. "Wish me luck at my first basketball practice!" I say to my cat. I've been spending all my spare time shooting baskets in my driveway. I really hope it has helped.

I adjust my ponytail and take one last look at myself in my mirror before I go.

I look ready. I just hope I'm ready for the Dream's first official practice.

Question of the day: Ready or NOT?

After what happened at tryouts, I can't help being a little bit nervous.

When I get to the basketball court, all the girls on my team are already there.

"Hi, Mallory," says Coach Darren in a loud voice. "We were waiting for you. Now we'll begin." He blows a whistle like he doesn't want to wait a minute longer.

"Sorry," I mumble. I can feel my face turning red. I make a note in my head to get to practices on time from now on.

Coach Darren motions for us to make a circle. "Girls, I'd like you to introduce yourselves. "Please tell us your name, what grade you're in, and one fun fact about yourself."

He turns to a tall girl on his left and nods for her to start.

"I'm Daisy. I'm in fifth grade, and I'm really excited for basketball season to start, but I'm not excited for it to end, because when it does, I have to get braces." She pretend-pouts and everyone laughs.

I rack my brain trying to decide what I'm going to say about myself. I could tell everyone I have a cat named Cheeseburger.

Coach Darren signals for the girl on Daisy's left to talk.

"I'm Amanda. Fifth grade." She pauses. "This is my first time playing basketball, and I'm not sure I'm going to be very good at it," she says quietly like she's embarrassed to admit it. "But I'm happy to be here."

When she says that, I see Arielle and Danielle look at each other like they're not so sure they're happy about having Amanda on their team. But *I'm* happy about it. She seems sweet—and even though I'm not sure I would say it out loud, I feel the same way she does.

"You're going to learn a lot," says Coach Darren. "And I have a feeling you will surprise yourself."

He points to Arielle, who is to Amanda's left.

She smiles. "My name is Arielle. I'm in fourth grade." She wraps an arm around Danielle, who is standing next to her. "This is my best friend, Danielle. We've always been into dancing, but now we're totally excited about playing basketball."

Then she points to Olivia. "That's my big sister. She's an awesome player, and she's been teaching Danielle and me everything she knows."

Danielle starts talking before Coach Darren even tells her to. "I'm Danielle. Fourth grade." She points to Arielle.

"Best friend of Arielle." Then she points her other hand in Olivia's direction. "Student of Olivia."

I look at Coach Darren. He said to give a fun fact about yourself, not yourself and your best friend. But he doesn't look like he minds that that's what Arielle and Danielle did.

"I'm glad to hear you girls have been working together to improve your basketball skills." He points to Olivia.

"My name is Olivia. I'm in fifth grade, and I'm totally psyched about playing basketball. I played in another league last year, and I can't wait to play in this one."

"Me too!" says a tall girl standing next to

her. "I'm Bree, fifth grade, and my brother plays on his high school team. He says he's coming to all my games, and I want to show him he's not the only one in our family who can play."

Coach Darren laughs. "A little family rivalry never hurts," he says. Even though he didn't say that everyone's fun facts should be about basketball, they have been. I try to think of something other than my cat.

"Hi, I'm Liz, and I'm in fourth grade," says a girl next to Bree. She must be from one of the other elementary schools, since I've never seen her before. "I love to play piano and tell jokes. I've never played a sport before, and I'm pretty sure I'm going to be terrible at it, but I'm excited to try."

I see Danielle and Arielle give each other a look like they need a good basketball player not a joke teller on their team.

But Coach Darren looks happy. "We look forward to hearing some of your jokes, and good for you for trying something new," he says to Liz. Then he nods at me.

"My name is Mallory. I'm in fourth grade, and I've never been on a team before, so I'm really excited to be here."

"We're excited to have you," says Coach Darren.

I watch Arielle and Danielle roll their eyes at each other like they're not as excited about it as Coach Darren is. I know they're thinking about what happened at tryouts, but I'm going to show them that I'm better than they think.

"We're going to do some warm-ups, stretching, and strengthening exercise," says Coach Darren. "Then we'll start working on shooting, dribbling, passing, and some basic plays so we can learn to work together as a team. I'll also be teaching you about the rules of the game. At the end of practice, I'm going to give you a take-home sheet with some basketball terms for you to learn."

He pauses like what he's about to say next is serious. "Girls, learning to play basketball is a process. It will be different for everyone. All I expect from each of you is to do your best and to be good teammates to each other."

Then he blows his whistle. "Fall in line!"
He motions for us to follow him as he starts
running laps around the court.

I keep up with the other girls on the
team as we finish our final lap around the
court.

"Good job!" says Coach Darren. Then
he leads us in a series of stretches and
explains that we'll do warm-ups and
stretches before each game.

I let out a deep breath as I bend down to
touch my toes. So far, so good.

When we're done stretching, Coach
Darren brings out a big mesh bag filled
with balls. "Girls, time for some dribbling,
passing, and shooting." He gives everyone
a ball and shows us proper dribbling
technique. Then we all dribble as we run up
and down the court.

It's easy to see that Bree and Olivia

are great. Daisy, Arielle, and Danielle are good too. But when I try to dribble the way Coach Darren showed us, the ball keeps going down the court faster than I do. The same thing happens to Liz and Amanda.

After a few minutes, Coach Darren blows a whistle and calls Liz, Amanda, and me over. "Girls, try it like this." He works with us while the other girls keep dribbling on the court.

"Why are basketball players messy eaters?" Liz asks Amanda and me as we work on the moves Coach Darren showed us.

"Why?" asks Amanda.

"Because they always dribble," answers Liz.

Amanda laughs like she appreciates Liz's basketball humor, and I like it too. But what I don't like is that the other girls are spending more time looking at the three of us than they are running their own drills, and the main ones who are looking are Arielle and Danielle.

The same thing happens when we start working on shooting and passing. Every time I shoot the ball, it goes somewhere other than the basket. And I don't know why.

Coach Darren calls Amanda, Liz, and me over again for "special instructions."

It doesn't seem to bother Amanda. "I knew

it was going to be hard for me to learn to play," she says.

Liz doesn't seem to mind it either. She keeps making jokes about missing baskets and where they might be. I can't help but laugh as she clowns around, but still, I wish I wasn't one of the players being pulled aside for extra help.

At home, when I practice, I make shots all the time. But I can't make any when we practice together as a team. Even Amanda and Liz make more baskets than I do.

This keeps happening all week. In third grade, my teacher, Mrs. Daily, taught us the expression "Practice makes perfect." But in my case, it's not working.

"Girls," says Coach Darren as the Dream huddles together at our last practice before our first game, "we play the Mystics this Saturday."

Danielle and Arielle both glance at me and give me an *I-hope-you've-got-what-it-takes-to-help-our-team-win* look. I try to give them a *yes-I-do* look as Coach Darren keeps talking.

"Get lots of rest, drink plenty of fluids, and come ready to play and win!" Coach Darren says.

Everyone claps, and then we put our hands together. "GO, DREAM!" we shout.

"GO, DREAM!" I shout with my teammates. Then I think, *Go, Mallory!* I really hope I have what it takes to help our team win.

GAME DAY

I feel like I'm going to throw up as Mom snaps my picture. "You'll always want to remember your first basketball game," she says with a smile.

I adjust the ribbon I tied around my ponytail to match my Dream jersey. I hope this game does turn out to be something I want to remember and not something I'd rather forget.

Last night at dinner, I tried to talk to

Dad about how I was feeling.

"It's normal to be nervous before a game," he said.

But I told Dad that what I was feeling wasn't just normal nerves. "I always make baskets when I practice at home, but I never make them at practice with my team. If that's what happens at practice, what do you think will happen during a real game?" I asked.

Dad didn't seem too concerned. "There's something called adrenaline," he told me. Then he explained that there's a chemical in everyone's body that kicks in when they're nervous and helps them perform better.

That made me feel a little bit better until Max chimed in. "There's also something called performance anxiety," he said. "Some people just fall apart under pressure."

That was definitely not what I wanted to hear.

But as nervous as I was last night, it can't compare to how I feel today. As I walk into the gym toward my team, the oatmeal I ate for breakfast does a somersault in my stomach. I make a quick wish that I play well and do my part to help my team win this game.

"Mallory!" I hear someone yell my name. Actually, it's two someones. Zoe and Grace run over to me. They're wearing their Mystics uniforms.

"I can't believe our team is playing your team for our first game," says Grace.

"Our coach said you have a really good team and that this is going to be a tough game," adds Zoe.

It should make me feel good to know that other teams have heard our team is good, but it makes me feel more nervous than ever. I don't want to be the player on our team that doesn't play well and ruins it for everyone else.

That thought stays in my brain the whole time our team warms up and stretches and even during our pregame team meeting.

"Bree, Olivia, Daisy, Arielle, and Danielle will be starting," Coach Darren says. He talks to each one of them about what positions they will be playing and who they will be guarding from the other team during the game.

Then he turns to Liz, Amanda, and me. "Girls, you need to be ready when I tell you to go in." A buzzer sounds just as he finishes explaining what we will need to do and what plays he's going to call for the game.

Even though I'm sitting on the bench as the starting players take their positions on the floor, I'm really nervous, like it's a tie game and I'm at the free throw line. Soon enough, I'm going to be on that floor too, and when I am, not only are my teammates and my friends on the other team going to see me play, but so are all the parents and kids in the gym.

The buzzer sounds again, and this time when it does, the players on the court spring into action.

"Go, Bree!" Coach Darren yells as she and another player jump for the ball at tip-off. Bree gets there first and passes the ball to Daisy, who passes to Olivia, who shoots and makes the first basket.

"That's it!" Coach Darren yells to the girls on the court.

Amanda, Liz, and I all jump to our feet.

"Go, Dream!" we yell as they run down the court and block the other team from making their shot.

Daisy gets the rebound and dribbles the ball down the court. She takes a shot, but a big player from the other team blocks her and she misses.

"That's OK," shouts Coach Darren.

"It looks a little scary out there," Amanda says to Liz and me. I don't want to admit it, but I agree. I hope playing won't be as scary as it looks.

"Why didn't Cinderella make the basketball team?" Liz asks us.

"Why?" I ask.

"Because she ran away from the ball."

Even though Liz's joke is dumb, I can't help but smile. Amanda does too. I know Liz is just trying to help us both feel less nervous.

As the game continues, Amanda, Liz,

and I cheer from the bench and I start to relax a little. The Mystics aren't bad, but our team is much better. By the end of the first quarter, the Dream leads 12–4, and at the end of the second quarter, the score is 22–8.

"Way to go, girls!" Coach Darren high-fives the players as they take the bench during halftime. "That was a great first half. We have a big lead!" Then he motions to Amanda, Liz, and me. "Girls, I'm going to put you in with Bree and Olivia when the second half starts."

Danielle and Arielle look at each other like they're disappointed that Coach Darren is taking them out of the game. But they don't get a chance to say anything, because Coach Darren starts passing out water from a cooler and going over the third-quarter plays.

When he's done, Bree takes a marker out of her gym bag and writes GO, DREAM on everyone's hands. I smile as she writes on mine. Just looking at her words makes me feel better.

But when the buzzer sounds and the third quarter starts, I feel like my stomach is falling out of my body.

The Mystics have the ball first and they score. Bree gets the rebound and passes the ball to Olivia. Then Olivia throws it to me. I catch it, but then I just stand there frozen like a block of ice. I try to remember

the play Coach Darren taught us, but I feel like a vacuum cleaner sucked all my basketball knowledge out of my head.

"Pass it to Amanda!" I hear someone yell.

But before I have a chance to do anything, one of the players on the Mystics steals the ball from me, dribbles down the court, and they score again. The players on the Mystics bench all yell and cheer. I look over at our bench and see Arielle and Danielle shaking their heads.

"That's OK," yells Coach Darren.

But it's not OK. The Mystics score three more times before we make another basket. Bree and Olivia don't pass any more balls to me for the rest of the quarter. And even though Amanda and Liz don't make any baskets, they both do a good job passing the ball when it comes to them.

The third quarter ends, and the score is 26–16. The Dream is still ahead, but our lead is smaller. When Coach Darren takes Liz and me out and puts Arielle and Danielle back in, I'm actually relieved. I watch as the game ends and we win 32–24.

"Good job!" says Coach Darren. He has us line up, and we congratulate all the girls on the Mystics.

"Good game," Zoe says when we pass each other.

"Yeah, good game," says Grace.

"Thanks," I say. It was a good game, but I don't feel like I did anything to make it good.

And I know I'm not the only one who feels that way.

Even though Coach Darren calls a team meeting after we're done congratulating the other team and tells us what a good job we did, I can just imagine what Arielle and Danielle are thinking but not saying.

"Congratulations on your win," says Dad as we leave gym and walk toward the car.

"I didn't do anything to help our team win," I mumble.

He loops an arm around me. "It was your first game," he says.

I shrug like that doesn't make it any better.

Dad squeezes my shoulders. "Mallory, you're new to this. Give it some time. Remember how hard you worked to learn your lines when you had the starring role in *Annie*."

"That's different," I tell Dad. "Memorizing lines wasn't as hard as playing basketball."

Dad opens the car door for me, and I get in.

"Do you remember how much you had to practice before you learned how to play the tuba?" Dad asks when he gets into the car.

Actually, I do remember that. I had to work very hard.

Maybe Dad is right, and all I need to do is keep working hard at basketball. Maybe if I work very hard, I will play better in the next game. As Dad starts the car, I let out a big breath. Then I think about the Cinderella joke Liz made during the game.

I don't know where Cinderella found her fairy godmother, but I could really use her too.

THE LONGEST SEASON

I take a black marker off my desk
and put a fat *X* through the day on my
calendar. These past few weeks have flown
by. I can't believe today was the last game
of the regular season. Even though there
were only five games in our season, I feel
like it was the longest season ever.

In some ways, it has been a good
season. The Dream won all of our games,

and we're going to the playoffs. I'm happy about that. I'm also happy because I've gotten to be good friends with some of the girls on the team, especially Liz and Amanda. But there's something I'm not happy about.

In all five games we played, I DID NOT SCORE ONE POINT!

And trust me when I tell you I'm not the only one who noticed. If you don't believe me, keep reading and you'll see what I mean.

Game 1:

When our team played the Mystics, I didn't make any points. The only

thing I did was get the ball once, and then it got stolen from me. When it happened, no one said anything about it, but I saw Arielle and Danielle shake their heads like they couldn't believe I didn't pass the ball.

I kind of hoped they would just forget about it. But that wasn't the case.

At practice before the second game, Arielle said, "Mallory, you know we're playing against the Storm this Saturday."

"They're supposed to be really good," added Danielle.

I knew what they were really saying is that I needed to play my best at the game to help our team win. "I get it," I said.

But they must not have believed me.

"When you get the ball, pass it," said Arielle.

"And if you get it and you're near the basket, shoot it," said Danielle.

There wasn't much I could say to that. I knew they were right. All I could do was hope that when the second game rolled around, I would play better than I did in the first game.

Game 2:
But when the second game rolled around, I didn't play better.

Well, maybe I played a little better. When I got the ball, I passed it, but when I tried to shoot it, it went everywhere but in the basket.

After the game, a lot of people had a lot to say about how I played.

Danielle said I should eat, sleep, and breathe basketball. Arielle said I didn't need to do those things, but that when we have a game, I should try to play basketball. Coach Darren said he would help me with some extra shooting drills. April, who is on the Storm, asked me if I wanted to come to her house and do some extra practicing with her.

Even Mary Ann had something to say. She and Chloe Jennifer and Joey came to watch the game, and when it was over, Mary Ann gave me

some advice. "When you shoot, aim for just above the basket," she said.

I gave her a *how-can-you-have-an-opinion-when-you-don't-even-play* look. All Mary Ann did was shrug. "I'm just trying to be helpful," she said.

But to be honest, I didn't think Mary Ann was being all that helpful.

Game 3:

The third game, against the Liberty, was even worse for me than the first or the second game.

HOME 28   00:00   GUEST 17
PERIOD 4

At the first two games, Amanda didn't make a basket and neither did Liz. Even though part of me wanted everyone on my team to play the best that they could, another part of me was kind of relieved that there were two people on my team who played just as badly as I did.

But all that changed in the second half of our game against Liberty.

Amanda scored once, and Liz scored three times! I was the only one on my team who didn't make a basket.

When the game was over, Coach Darren said Liz was the Most Improved Player.

Everyone hugged her, and Daisy gave her a new nickname: Liz the Whiz. Everyone

was chanting, "Liz, Liz, basketball whiz."

Even though I was happy my team won and especially happy for Liz, all I could think about was that I had to improve before the next game.

When I got home from the game, I went to the wish pond and made a wish that I would score in the next game. I even threw an extra wish pebble in the wish pond for good luck.

Game 4:

Apparently, the wish pebble I threw in the wish pond for good luck didn't

work. During Game 4 against the Sparks, I didn't score one single point.

I tried. I got the ball and shot it three times. Once it came close and almost went

in, but it didn't. In our team meeting after the game, Coach Darren said he was really proud of our team. "Four straight wins!" he said. Then he said what he thought each player did well during the game.

He said that Olivia, Bree, and Daisy, who scored a combined total of eighteen of our twenty-six points, are all team leaders and played great.

He said Arielle, who scored four points, did her part to help us beat the Sparks.

He said Danielle, who made two steals, was really on her game.

Then he high-fived Liz and Amanda, who each made one basket, and said they really stepped up their games and did a great job.

When he got to me, all he said was that my passing and dribbling had improved. I know they have, and I know those are important skills. But he didn't say what I would have liked him to have said, which was, "Good job scoring."

Game 5:

The game today against the Fever was really close. We

almost lost, but in the last few seconds of the game, Olivia made a three-point shot, and we won our final game of the regular season. Everyone in the stands went crazy! Even though I hadn't made any points, it was really exciting to win.

After the game, Coach Darren gave our team a long talk about what a great season we had and how we need to really work hard as a team so we do well in the playoffs.

Unfortunately, Coach Darren wasn't the only one who had something to say about the playoffs. When the team meeting was over, Arielle and Danielle caught up with me on the way out of the gym.

"Mallory, now that we're in the playoffs, it's really important that you work on your shooting," said Danielle.

"This game is super important to us," said Arielle.

"That means you need to try your hardest to score," added Danielle.

Amanda overheard what they said. "Mallory is trying her hardest," she said. Then she reminded Arielle and Danielle what Coach Darren said at the start of the season about doing your best AND being good teammates. It was really nice of Amanda to stand up for me. It made me feel a little better. But the truth is that everyone on my team wants to win the playoffs, and I do too.

I just don't get why I can't score during games. I make plenty of baskets when I shoot hoops in my driveway. I've even improved at practice with my team. The problem I have is that I get nervous when we play games. Maybe Max put a curse on me when he told me about performance anxiety.

Is she CURSED?

Either way, the playoffs are in a week and I know I need to do something.

The only question is, WHAT?!?

THE GIRL WHO NEVER SCORED

By Mallory McDonald

Once upon a time there was a sweet, cute girl with red hair and freckles who decided to play basketball on a team. She made the decision to do this even though her best friends didn't want to do it with her. She had always wanted to be part of a team, and she knew this was her chance. She was really excited to play, but once she got on a team, there was a problem.

The problem was that the girl couldn't make a basket.

It wasn't like she wasn't trying.

She went to all the practices. She did what her coach told her to do. She did extra things like practicing with a friend who played on another team. She even tried to follow the advice of her best friend, who hadn't signed up to play basketball but had an opinion on how to play it anyway, and tried to aim for just above

The girl who **never** SCORED!!

the basket when she took a shot.

But no matter what she did, when she shot the ball, it didn't go in the basket. This bothered the girl, and it bothered some of the girls on her team too—especially when the team made it to the playoffs. Even though the girls on the team had wanted to win their other games, they really wanted to win the playoffs. And they told the sweet, cute girl with red hair and freckles exactly how they felt about it.

One of them said to her, "This game is SUPER important to us."

Another girl said, "That means you need to try your hardest to score."

It bothered the girl that the other girls said these things because she knew the game was SUPER important and she HAD been trying her hardest to score.

HONEST, but **NOT** very nice teammates.

But in her heart, she knew what the girls were saying was true (even though she didn't think that it was very nice that they said it). She was the only girl on the team who hadn't scored, and she knew that for her team to win the playoffs, she needed to try even harder.

She needed to score some points!

So she decided to talk to someone else who might be able to help her.

She talked to her brother.

At first, when she told him her

problem, he wasn't very helpful. He said that all the athletic talent in the family must have gone to him and maybe she should go back to doing things she's good at like watching fashion shows on TV.

But when she told her mother what he said, he got in trouble and his mother made him promise to help her.

So he did.

They shot hoops together in their driveway. They did push-ups and sit-ups in his room.

He even gave her some helpful advice. "When you play, just stay calm. Think of a word that helps you relax and keep saying that word."

He even helped the girl think of the word she would use.

The girl was starting to feel a little bit better about how she would play during the upcoming semifinal game. But just to be sure, the morning of the semifinal game, she called one more person who she knew could help her. She called her lifelong best friend, who came over to her house right away and was VERY helpful.

She brushed the girl's hair into a special semifinal hairstyle. She did a cartwheel and a handstand and a good-luck cheer. She even let the girl wear her lucky butterfly socks.

When she was done, she gave the girl a big hug and told her that she would be at the game to watch her play and that she KNEW she would score.

The girl felt a lot better, but still, she wasn't going to take any chances.

So, before she left for the game, she made a quick trip to the wish pond

on her street. She picked up a pebble, squeezed her eyes shut tight, and made a wish.

"I wish I will score a basket."

When she was done wishing, the sweet, cute girl with red hair and freckles opened her eyes and smiled. She felt ready to play!

DISASTER AT THE GYM

All the confidence I felt this morning at the wish pond is gone. Just about everyone I know or have ever known is in this gym— Mom, Dad, Max, Mary Ann, Joey, Chloe Jennifer, and lots of kids from my school.

"Good luck, Sweet Potato," Dad says.

Mom wraps her arm around me. "I'm sure the Dream will win," she says with a smile.

I look at Max.

"Relax," says my brother. "Just remember what I told you. Stay calm and use your word."

"Good luck," says Joey.

"You'll do great," says Chloe Jennifer.

"You're ready!" says Mary Ann. She points to the lucky socks on my feet. "You've got everything you need to score!"

But as Coach Darren calls our team together for our pregame meeting, I don't feel relaxed or ready. While he reviews the plays we will use, I feel like the butterflies flew off Mary Ann's socks and into my stomach.

As Coach Darren talks, people keep coming in to the gym. It's standing room only.

A choir group from the high school sings the National Anthem. Then Coach Nelson, who is wearing the same sweat

suit she had on during tryouts, takes the microphone.

"Welcome to the Fern Falls Girls Basketball League playoffs," she says. "All of the teams in the league have done a fabulous job. This morning, the Dream will play the Mystics, and then the Storm will play the Fever in the semifinal games of the season. The winners of both games will face off in the finals next weekend. Good luck to all four teams!"

After she says that, a buzzer sounds signaling that it's time for the game to begin.

Amanda, Liz, and I watch from the bench as the rest of the girls on our team run to their positions on the court for the tip-off.

I look over at the Mystics bench. Grace is on it, but Zoe is in the game as a starter. I watch as she makes the first basket of the game. The crowd in the bleachers claps and cheers.

"Go!" Coach Darren yells as Daisy gets the rebound. She passes the ball to Bree, who passes it to Olivia, who shoots and scores.

Amanda, Liz, and I all jump up and start cheering. We keep cheering through the whole first quarter. Even though we beat the Mystics the last time we played them, they've improved a lot. The game is tied 8–8 at the end of the first quarter

When the second quarter ends, we're ahead, but just by two points.

At halftime, Coach Darren gives our team what he calls a *motivational talk*. I can tell Coach Darren wants to make it to the finals just as much as we do.

"Girls, let's get the job done!" he says.

We all put our hands together. "GO, DREAM!" we shout.

When the buzzer sounds for the start of the second half, Coach Darren puts Liz and Amanda in. Then he looks at me. "Mallory, get ready; you're up next."

I think about the wish I made at the wish pond. I really hope I make a basket when it's my turn to play. I watch as the two teams on the court fight for the ball. It looks more like a battle than a basketball game.

BATTLE of the BASKET!

Coach Darren is yelling plays to our team, and the coach of the Mystics is yelling plays to her team. Everyone in the crowd is clapping and cheering.

When the third quarter ends, the score is tied 18–18.

"OK, Mallory, you're in," says Coach Darren as the fourth quarter begins. When I get in position on the court, I make eye contact with Grace, who also just got put in the game. I can't tell if she's nervous or not, but I know I am.

I think about Max's advice. I just need to stay calm. I take a deep breath and silently say my word.

Cheeseburger.

The Dream gets the ball first. Daisy passes it to Arielle.

"Go, Dream!" I hear the girls on my team yell from the bench.

I look over at Arielle. I know she's trying to figure out who she can pass the ball to, but it's not easy. All the rest of the players on my team are being blocked.

I run to the side of the court. "I'm open!" I yell to Arielle.

Arielle looks around to see who else on our team might be open, but no one is. She hesitates and then passes me the ball.

Cheeseburger.

This is my chance! I run to the basket with the ball. As I run, I can hear people on my team yelling, but it's hard to hear what they're yelling. As I near the basket, I don't even stop to think; I just shoot.

Go in! Go in! Go in! I say silently to the ball. I watch as it arches up and soars through the net. I made a basket! I can't believe it. My wish came true! My word worked!

I look over at Coach Darren. I can't wait to see him give me a thumbs-up for a job well done, but what I see is him giving the time-out signal.

I can't imagine why he's calling a time-out.

I look at the referee, but he just shakes his head like it's not his job to explain this to me.

Maybe Coach Darren is so happy he doesn't want to wait until the end of the game to tell me how proud he is of me. He knows the other girls will be happy and want to congratulate me too. Everyone knows I've been upset about not scoring. But as I walk toward our bench, Coach Darren doesn't look too happy and neither do the other girls on my team.

"Way to go, Mallory," says Danielle—but not like she means it.

"You scored in the other team's basket," says Arielle. "Now they're ahead by two points!"

Danielle slaps her forehead like she shouldn't have to explain what happened to me. "Didn't you hear us yelling? We were saying, 'Wrong way, Mallory!'"

"What?" I shake my head. I don't understand. I look at Coach Darren.

"I'm sorry, Mallory," he says. "You went the wrong way. You scored in the other team's basket, so they get the points."

Everyone on my team is looking at me and not in a nice way. I look back at the referee, who is still on the court. But he looks away like he knows what happened and doesn't want to make me feel worse than I already do.

I can't believe I got confused and ran the wrong way.

I think about the advice Max gave me. He told me to stay calm when I play. He told me to use my word. I tried and it helped me score but in the wrong basket! I can only imagine what he's going to say when we get home. He's probably embarrassed that we're in the same family.

All of a sudden, the gym feels way too warm. Tears are starting to well up in my eyes.

Coach Darren can tell I'm upset. "Don't worry about it, Mallory. Mistakes happen."

"It was a great shot," says Liz.

Amanda wraps an arm around me. "It went right through the net."

"Yeah," mumbles Arielle.

"The other team's net," adds Danielle.

"Girls!" says Coach Darren. His voice sounds sharper than usual. "We need to come together as a team. There's plenty of time on the clock. We can still win this game."

"I don't know about that," says Arielle.

"This is a disaster," says Danielle.

"Let's not be dramatic," says Coach Darren.

But for once, I agree with Danielle. This is a disaster, and it's all my fault.

A PEP TALK

When I wake up and open my eyes, the first thing I remember is how horrible yesterday was. We won the game against the Mystics—but not because of anything I did.

I tried hard, but nothing I did helped. Not the extra practices or drills or even Mary Ann's lucky socks. I couldn't even follow the advice my brother gave me and stay calm. If I had, I wouldn't have run the wrong way, scored for the other team, and made my teammates upset with me.

I pull Cheeseburger in next to me, close my eyes, and try not to think about it. But it's all I can think about. When I open my eyes again, I have an idea.

Actually, it's not an idea. It's a decision. I'm going to quit.

What's the use in playing if I'm not helping my team win?

I think about Mom and Dad. I know they'll say that once you start something, you shouldn't quit. But in this case, I'll be doing my team a favor if I do. I can just imagine how relieved they'll be when they find out.

The only thing I need to do now is tell Coach Darren. We have a special practice this afternoon so we're ready for the final game. I'm going to go early and tell Coach Darren before the rest of the girls even show up. Then I won't have to see Arielle and Danielle and the others celebrating when they find out I'm not on the team anymore.

"Coach Darren, may I talk to you?" I say as soon as I get to the gym. Even though what I have to say isn't easy, I start talking right away. I want to get this over with. "I've been doing a lot of thinking since the game yesterday, and what I think is that I'm no help to this team."

Coach Darren opens his mouth like he's about to say something, but I don't give him a chance. "I quit," I say. I hand Coach Darren my jersey to show him I'm serious.

I wait for him to high-five me or take my jersey or breathe a big sigh of relief, but he doesn't do any of those things. What he says is "Mallory, you can't quit."

I was hoping he wasn't going to say that, but I came prepared in case he did. "There are lots of reasons why I should quit," I tell Coach Darren. I pull the list I made out of my back pocket and start reading.

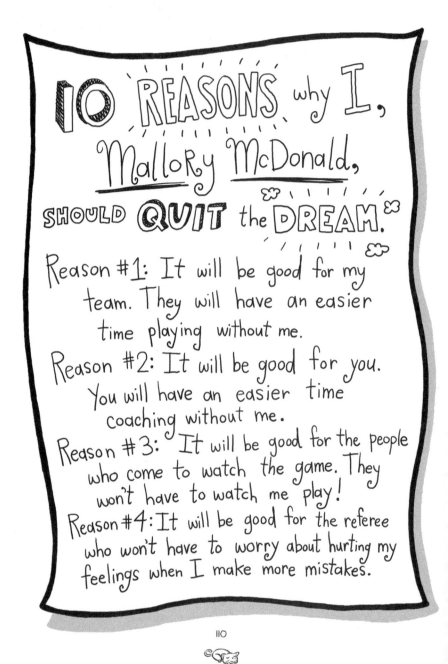

10 REASONS why I, Mallory McDonald, SHOULD QUIT the DREAM.

Reason #1: It will be good for my team. They will have an easier time playing without me.

Reason #2: It will be good for you. You will have an easier time coaching without me.

Reason #3: It will be good for the people who come to watch the game. They won't have to watch me play!

Reason #4: It will be good for the referee who won't have to worry about hurting my feelings when I make more mistakes.

Reason #5: It will be good for my parents who won't have to give me any more speeches about how they're proud of me for trying something new (even though I stink at it!)

Reason #6: It will be good for my brother who won't be embarrassed again by my horrible playing.

Reason #7: It will be good for my best friend who will get her lucky socks back.

Reason #8: It will be good for Fashion Fran who will get one of her loyal viewers back.

Reason #9: It will be good for the reputation of the Fern Falls Girls' Basketball League.

Reason #10: If I quit, the Dream will have a better chance of winning the championship!

When I'm done reading, I wait for Coach Darren to say he gets it. But instead, he says, "Mallory, I know how badly you wanted to make a basket. It's a shame you scored in the wrong hoop, but that's not a reason to quit."

Coach Darren might not think it is, but I do. Plus, I just gave him ten other reasons.

"It's not that simple," I say. "I'm no good, and I'm not the only one who thinks so."

Coach Darren shakes his head. "Is this about what happened at the game yesterday?"

Even though he doesn't come out and say it, I know Coach Darren is talking about what Arielle and Danielle said after I scored in the wrong basket.

I look down at the toes of my basketball shoes.

Coach Darren sits down on a bench.

I sit down next to him. "You can't worry about what other people think. Just focus on your own game. Remember, a great team isn't just a team made up of the best players. A great team is made up of players who care about each other, try their best, and enjoy what they're doing. Even if you never score a single point for us, you're still part of what makes our team great."

I think Coach Darren can tell I'm not convinced. He keeps talking.

"When the season started, I said that learning to play basketball takes a different amount of time for each player. I said that all I expected from this team was for all of you to do your best and be good teammates to each other. I'm going to have a talk with the team today and remind them about what I said."

"It's not their fault I haven't helped them win," I say.

"Mallory, team sports aren't just about winning. They're about knowing that you tried your best and that you had fun too."

I think about that for a minute.

"I definitely tried my hardest," I say to Coach Darren. I think about Liz's jokes and how sweet Amanda has been and the fun times I've had during practices and games. "And I've had fun playing this season and getting to know some of the girls on the team too."

Coach Darren smiles like he likes my answer. Then he gets a serious look on his face. "Mallory, you've learned a lot this season. Your dribbling and passing have improved, and your shooting has too."

He looks me in the eye like what he's about to say next is very important. "It's not uncommon to get nervous in a game, especially an important one. Focus on the positive. You made a basket. You can do it again, and I'm certain that the next time you try, it will be in the right basket."

I look up at Coach Darren. "Thanks for the pep talk, but how can you be so certain?"

Coach Darren smiles again. "I've been around this game for a long time. I started playing when I was a little kid. Stick with it. Your moment will come. All you need to do is stay in the game."

"You really think so?" I ask Coach Darren.

"I know so," he says.

V IS FOR VICTORY!

Today is game day!

It's the final game against the Fever. I bend down and pick up the shiniest pebble I can find. Then I squeeze my eyes shut and toss it into the wish pond.

I wish that this will be a good game for me. I want to make a basket; I really do. But the truth is that I know there's more to basketball than just being a great player.

Once everyone showed up for our special practice the other day, Coach Darren talked to the team, just like he said he was going to do. But he wasn't the only one who had something to say.

So did Amanda. She said that she felt badly about how upset I was at the semifinal game and that she didn't think "people" were as nice as they should have been. When she said "people," she looked right at Arielle and Danielle. Then Bree looked at them and said she felt the same way too.

I was really surprised when they said that, but I was even more surprised at what happened next.

Olivia looked at Arielle and Danielle, and they nodded at each other like they had something to say and it was time to say it.

"Mallory, I'm sorry if I got carried away

at the semifinal game," said Arielle.

"Me too," said Danielle. Then she looked at me like she really meant what she said next. "And I'm sorry if I haven't been so nice this season."

Arielle nodded like she was part of that apology too. "We're a team, and we're in this together."

When she said that, Olivia nodded at Arielle and Danielle like they had talked about what happened and she was proud of them for what they'd said.

It definitely made me feel better. I could tell that Arielle and Danielle really did feel bad and that they meant what they said.

"Thanks," I said to them both. "I'm glad we're on the same team."

Then Daisy said that we'd talked enough and that it was time to practice. So that's what we did, and hopefully we're ready because today's the big game!

As Coach Nelson welcomes everyone, I think about my talk with Coach Darren. He sounded so certain that he knew what he was talking about when he said I could do it. I just hope he's right!

I look around the gym. It's even more packed than the day of the semifinals.

This morning at breakfast, Max told me to block out everything that's going on except for what my coach tells me and what's happening on the court. That's what I'm going to have to do. I don't have a choice.

"Olivia, Bree, Daisy, Liz, and Mallory, you're starting!" Coach Darren announces at the beginning of our pregame meeting.

My mouth falls open. I wasn't expecting him to put me in, and I don't think anyone else was either. I look at Arielle and

Danielle. Even after what they said, I still expect them to shake their heads and roll their eyes. But they don't.

Arielle pats me on the back. "You got it," she says.

Danielle gives me a thumbs-up like she thinks so too.

As the buzzer signals the beginning of the game, Coach Darren gives me a *you-can-do-it* look. I run to my position on the court.

At tip-off, a Fever player gets the ball. She dribbles it down the court and makes the first basket.

The gym fills with clapping and cheering. I look up in the stands and see someone holding a sign that says, *GO FEVER!*

Daisy gets the rebound and passes the ball to Olivia, who passes it to me. *Focus, Mallory. Stay calm.* I pass the ball to Bree. There's more clapping and cheering as she scores.

As the Fever and the Dream go back and forth

across the court, I can feel myself starting to relax into the rhythm of the game. I make another pass to Daisy when the ball comes to me and she scores.

When the first quarter ends, the score is tied 10–10. Coach Darren takes out Liz and me and puts in Arielle and Danielle.

"Good job, Mallory," Coach Darren says as I take the bench.

I didn't get a chance to shoot, but I feel pretty happy that I made two good passes.

The second quarter is pretty much a repeat of the first. Both teams battle it out, and when the quarter ends, the score is tied 18–18.

"We're playing a tough team," Coach Darren says as we huddle during halftime. "We're going to have to step up our playing if we want to pull ahead in the second half."

He puts Arielle, Amanda, Danielle, Bree, and Daisy in as the second half begins.

But the third quarter doesn't go as well as the first two. The Fever score right away. Danielle gets the rebound and passes it to Bree, who dribbles it down the court but misses her layup. The Fever score again. Then Arielle misses the next shot.

The Fever pull ahead, and by the end of the third quarter, they're up 28–22.

"Girls, we need to give this our all!" Coach Darren says. "Mallory, you're in." He motions for me to take Amanda's spot.

I take a deep breath. It wasn't so hard to stay calm and focused in the first quarter when the game was tied and there was still plenty of time for us to win, but now we're down by six, and we need to make a comeback if we're going to win the game.

I look at Coach Darren.

"You can do it," he says.

I nod and run to the court.

The Dream gets the ball first. Amanda gets the ball and passes it to me.

I pass the ball to Daisy, who takes it to the basket and scores. A player on the Fever gets the ball and misses her shot. I hear my teammates yelling from the bench.

They keep yelling as we score again. The Fever score too. The crowd is going crazy. The two teams battle it out, and with less than a minute to go, Olivia shoots and it's a tie game.

Coach Darren calls a time-out. We huddle in close as he goes over what will probably be our last play of the game.

"When you go back out, the Fever has the ball," says Coach Darren. "They're going to try to hold for the last shot. Stick to your girl and play tight defense and hopefully they won't score."

He looks at the five of us like the success of the season is resting on our shoulders. "Arielle, Amanda, and Mallory, if you get the ball, pass it to Daisy or Bree so they can shoot. Remember, we only have time for one basket. Let's make it count."

We put our hands together. "GO,

DREAM!" we shout as we run back into the game.

When the Fever get the ball, they hold just like what Coach Darren said they would. When their player with the ball finally tries to shoot, Bree blocks her and she misses.

The gym feels like it's shaking because there's so much yelling and cheering.

Arielle gets the rebound and passes it to Daisy. She dribbles it as she runs toward our basket. I glance up at the clock. There are just twelve seconds left to shoot.

"Go, Daisy!" I hear the rest of our team yell from the bench.

If our team makes a basket, we win. If we don't, this game goes into overtime.

I watch Daisy as she tries to dribble and get close to the basket, but a player on the other team is blocking her. She can't shoot.

There are only eight seconds left.

"Pass it to Mallory! She's open!" Coach Darren yells.

Daisy looks at me and throws the ball my way. I catch it and start to dribble toward the basket.

"GO, Mallory!" I hear my team yell.

I know there are just a few seconds left on the clock. It's now or never. I shoot the ball, but I miss because a player on the Fever knocks into me.

The referee blows his whistle and calls a foul on the Fever.

Everyone freezes. There are only two seconds left. It's a tie game, and I'm going to the free throw line. I will get two chances to make a basket.

Coach Darren calls another time-out. He motions me over. "Mallory, just pretend you're at practice. You can make this shot."

He pats me on the shoulder. "Go get 'em," he says as I head back to the court.

When I get to the free throw line, I take a deep breath. I can't believe this all comes down to me. I bend my knees, take a deep breath, and shoot.

The ball comes close but doesn't touch the net. I groan. I can't believe I missed.

"It's OK," says Bree, who is to my right. "You still have one more shot."

"Go, Mallory!" I hear my teammates chanting from the bench.

I think about what Coach Darren told me about being patient and what Max said about staying calm. The referee hands me the ball. I try to block out everything but the basket in front of me. The gym is silent as I bend my knees and shoot.

The ball arches toward the basket.

Go in. Go in. Go in.

I watch as the ball circles the rim and then drops through the basket. The crowd goes crazy.

One of the players on the Fever gets the rebound, runs to the center of the court and throws up a desperation shot.

But the buzzer sounds before the ball gets anywhere near their basket. The game is officially over.

"We won!" screams Daisy.

Suddenly the whole team is on the court and hugging and high-fiving, and the main person they're hugging is me.

"Mallory, you did it!" says Amanda. "You made the winning basket."

"Awesome shot!" screams Arielle.

The next thing I know, Coach Darren is at my side. He gives me a high five. "Great job, Mallory! I knew you could do it!" he says. "I'm so proud of you!"

I'm proud of myself too. I can't believe the Dream won the championship and I made the winning basket.

It's all I can think about as we congratulate the girls on the Fever for playing a great game. I'm still thinking about it as Coach Nelson presents Coach Darren with a big team trophy and hands out individual trophies to the players on our team. When she gives me my trophy, I smile. It's the first trophy I've ever won.

The gym fills with applause, and a photographer comes to the floor to take our official championship photo.

When he's done taking our picture,

Coach Darren calls everyone on our team together. "I'm proud of all of you," he says. "Winning the championship was great, but knowing that we came together and worked as a team is even better."

I agree with Coach Darren. As happy as I am about winning the game, I'm even happier that I'm a part of this team. We worked together to win, and it feels great.

The next thing I know, all our families and friends are on the floor of the gym congratulating us. Dad gives me a big hug and so does Mom, and Max high-fives me.

"Time to celebrate!" says Coach Darren.

Amanda's mom brought confetti, and Olivia and Arielle's mom has a cake with a big *V* on it. "*V* is for Victory!" she says.

"How did you know we would be victorious?" Olivia asks.

Her mom smiles. "Mother's intuition," she says.

My mom takes pictures while we all throw confetti and eat cake and celebrate our victory.

As the celebration dies down and everyone starts to leave the gym, there's someone I need to talk to. I go over to Coach Darren. "Thanks for getting me to hang in there," I tell him.

Coach Darren smiles.

"I just have one question," I add. "Why did you put me in the most important game at the most important time?" I ask.

I know he gets what I'm NOT saying, which is that it was kind of surprising since I'm not one of the best players. Coach Darren smiles. "Mallory, I told you that I've been around this game for a long time. I put you in because I knew you could do it."

"Thanks," I say again. His answer makes me feel really good.

I think back to the day the letter came about playing in the league. When I said I wanted to play, Max told me that being on a team isn't all fun and games. He was right about that. First, my best friends didn't want to play with me. Then I was put on a team with people I didn't want to be with. And no matter what I did, I couldn't make a basket. But still, a lot of it was fun. I learned so much and made so many new friends. Plus, the Dream are league champions!

I made a lot of wishes during basketball season. Some of them came true, and some of them didn't. Playing basketball wasn't always easy, but I'm so glad I stuck with it.

The bottom line: I feel like a champ. Both on the court and off.

ANOTHER WIN

"Please pass the pepperoni to put on the pizza," says Daisy.

Liz and Amanda look at each other and burst out laughing.

"That sounds like a tongue twister," says Bree. Everyone starts saying it together, and the next thing I know, the whole team is cracking up. We keep laughing while Liz tells what I'm sure is the worst basketball joke ever.

"What do you call a pig that plays basketball?' she asks.

"A ball hog!" she says before anyone even asks. Laughter fills up my kitchen.

I look at Mom. "Thanks!" I mouth to her. She winks at me. I'm really glad she let me invite everyone over to make pizzas. She knows how awful I felt after I made a basket in the wrong goal during the semifinal game, and she knows that I really wanted to quit. She and Dad both told me after the final game when the Dream won that they were so proud of me for sticking with basketball. I know they get how much it means to me to have all the girls on the team over to my house to celebrate.

"OK, girls," says Mom. "Let's see how creative you can get with these pizzas."

When everyone is done putting sauce and cheese on their crusts, Mom passes around bowls of onions and green peppers and other pizza toppings I helped her chop earlier this morning.

"Look at mine," says Bree. She holds up a pizza with "#1" on it made out of mushrooms.

Danielle has a "#1" on her pizza too, but hers is made out of onions. Olivia and Daisy put pepperonis on their pizzas and decorate them with shreds of basil so

that they look like basketballs. Liz makes
a smiley face out of black olives, and
Amanda makes an exclamation mark out
of green peppers.

"Check out this," says Arielle. Her pizza
has a *V* on it made out of pepperoni. *V* is
for victory," she says.

"Mallory, I like your pizza," says Liz. I
hold up the pizza I made which has a *D*
for Dream on it made
out of basil leaves
surrounded by a heart
made out of olives.

When everyone
finishes decorating
the pizzas, Mom slides
them into the oven.

I think about asking the girls if they want
to shoot some baskets in my driveway, but
I feel like I've shot enough baskets lately.

"Who wants to watch TV while our pizzas are cooking?" I ask.

Everyone likes that idea. We pile onto the couch in the den, and I click on the TV. We watch a reality show about some kids in a cooking contest. They're making roasted duck with wild cherries, rice pilaf with almonds and asparagus, and chocolate mousse for dessert.

"I personally think our pizzas look better," says Daisy.

"Much better!" says Bree. Everyone agrees, and when we hear the buzzer go off in the kitchen, we race back to see if our pizzas taste as good as they smell. All the girls on my team ooh and aah as Mom takes the pizzas out of the oven.

"Wow!" says Amanda. "They look so good!"

Mom lines the pizzas up on the counter so we can all take a look.

"We should take pictures," says Olivia. The next thing I know, everyone who has phones has them out and is taking pictures. Mom gets her camera out and takes some too.

"Who's ready to eat?" I ask when everyone is done taking pictures.

Olivia shakes her head like she's not ready. "We should have a contest to decide which one is the best."

"Who would be the judge?" asks Bree.

Everyone looks at Mom like she would be the only fair choice.

"Oh no!" Mom laughs. "I couldn't possibly choose, but you guys can."

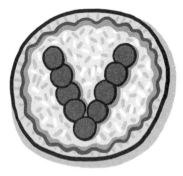

She passes around pieces of paper and pencils. "Why don't you all write down which pizza you like best? Then we'll see which one gets the most votes."

We all get busy writing, and then we pass the little scraps of paper to Mom. She reads the results out loud. "One vote for Arielle's pizza with the *V* on it."

Mom unfolds the next scrap of paper. "One vote for Liz's smiley face."

Mom keeps reading the results. "A vote for Mallory," she says. Then she unfolds another scrap of paper. And another. And another. And another. She unfolds all the rest of the scraps of paper, and they all say the same thing. Almost everyone voted for me!

Mom grins. "Mallory, your Dream pizza is the clear winner."

Everyone claps. "Take a bow," says Daisy.

I do. Then I hold up my pizza while Mom takes a picture.

I can't believe it. First, I made the winning basket of the championship game. Now, I've won the pizza-making contest!

"Victory speech from the winner," says Bree.

I think about the speech Coach Darren made after we won the game.

"I just want to say two things." I pause. I want my words to be just right, just like Coach Darren's.

"The first thing I want to say is that I'm really happy about winning. I don't mean the pizza contest. I mean the basketball championship. But I'm even happier that I was part of the Dream and got to be friends with all of you."

They clap like they like my speech and feel the same way I do.

"What's the second thing?" asks Liz when the clapping stops.

I grin. This part is easier to say. "Let's eat!"

A SCRAPBOOK

Mary Ann and I have always made scrapbooks of fun activities that we've done together. Even though Mary Ann didn't play basketball with me, I still made a basketball scrapbook so I would remember all the highlights of the Dream's winning season. Here are a few of my favorite photos:

Here's the picture that Mom took of me in my uniform before the first game.

That day, I had no idea what to expect. Now, I feel like a basketball pro. Well, maybe not. But I definitely know more than I did when I started.

Here's the official Dream picture we took with Coach Darren when we won the championship game. It was such an exciting day. Even if I didn't have this picture to remember it, I know it's a day I'll never forget.

` Here's the unofficial picture we took when we celebrated our win! Just looking at it makes me happy. I think it will always be one of the happiest days of my life.

Last but not least, here's a picture of me with the girls from the team when they came over to make pizzas. I don't think I'll grow up to be a basketball player (though I might be a pizza maker!). But being part of this team was great, and I'm so glad I did it!

BASKETBALL LINGO

I'd be the first to admit that I learned a lot this season. I learned that even though it's not always easy, it's really fun and cool to be part of a team. And even if you're not the best player, you can still feel great about being part of the team, as long as you try your hardest.

I never thought I, Mallory McDonald, would be saying this, but now that the season is over, I'm kind of sad. I'll definitely miss playing basketball and hanging out with the girls on my team. I'll miss Coach Darren too. He taught me a lot—and not just that it's important to stick with it even when things are hard. He also taught me a lot of basketball lingo, so now when I go to a game or watch one on TV, I'll know what's happening.

Here are some of the most important terms I learned this season.

Coach Darren's Must-Know List of Basketball Terms
(with a few additional notes by Mallory McDonald)

assist: a pass to another basketball player that leads directly to a basket being made. It's also when you help someone do something, like chop ingredients to put on top of pizzas!

bench: the spot where the players who aren't playing sit during the game. There's also one by the wish pond (which comes in handy when I want to make a wish, and I made lots of them during the basketball season).

defense: the act of stopping the other team from scoring a basket. It's also what you use when your brother is being rude to you. For example,
MAX: You stink at basketball.
MALLORY: You just stink, especially your feet! Ha! Ha! Ha!

dribbling: the act of bouncing the basketball continuously. Another kind of dribbling is when water drips out of a faucet or spit drips out of your mouth (yuck!).

dunk: when a player jumps high, reaches above the rim, and stuffs the ball through the hoop. Also, it's when you stick a cookie into a glass of milk (which is a lot of fun to do!).

foul shot: an unopposed attempt to score points from the free throw line. It sounds like something stinky (like old cheese), but trust me, it's not—especially if you're the one making the foul shot in the final seconds of the championship game!

layup: a close-up shot taken after dribbling to the basket. You could also do what I call a lie-up. That's when you lie on the couch, put your feet up, and watch TV. A good time to do this would be on Saturday mornings when your favorite TV show is on (especially now that basketball season is over).

offense: the team with possession of the ball. Unfortunately, it can also mean when you do something wrong (like scoring in the other team's basket).

rebound: when a basketball player grabs a ball that is coming off the rim or backboard after missing a shot. It is also when you recover after making a mistake.

score: when you or someone on your team gets a ball in the basket and makes a point. It's a great thing! Especially when you're the one who does the scoring!

Now you know some of the most important terms in basketball. If you've never played, I hope you'll give it a try. It really is a lot of fun. And if you're a seasoned player, my only advice (in the words of Coach Darren) is to stay in the game!

Trust me, you won't regret it!

A RECIPE

Even if you don't play on a basketball team, making homemade pizzas with your friends is tons of fun and yummy too. Mom said that for the pizza to be truly homemade, we would have had to make our own crust and sauce. But my friends and I were more focused on what we put on top of 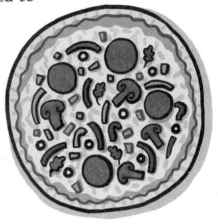 our pizzas, so we made what Mom calls almost homemade pizza. Here's the recipe:

Almost Homemade Individual Pizzas

Ingredients:

store-bought crusts (one individual-sized
  crust per person)

pizza sauce

shredded mozzarella cheese

toppings: pepperoni, canned mushrooms,
  canned black olives, chopped fresh
  basil, thinly sliced onions and green
  peppers, small chunks of pineapple,
  chopped ham

grated Parmesan cheese

Instructions:

Step 1: Preheat the oven to the
temperature shown on the pizza crust
package. Then put all your pizza
toppings and the pizza sauce in bowls
on your counter so that it will be easy

for your friends to get to them and share them. Make stations on your kitchen counter or table so everyone has a place to decorate a pizza.

Step 2: When your friends come over, give everyone a pizza crust. First, you will need to spread pizza sauce over your crust and then top it with a layer of shredded cheese. Then it is time to get creative and decorate! Your friends can cover their pizzas with any of these toppings. They can make shapes, letters, numbers, and anything else they can think of! The more creative, the better!

Step 3: Put your pizzas in the oven and bake according to the directions on the pizza crust package. While the pizzas are cooking, you can clean up the kitchen and help everyone get something to drink.

Step 4: When your pizzas are done cooking, sit down with your friends and enjoy hot, almost homemade, just out-of-the-oven pizza!

And one last thing: don't forget to take lots of pictures!

Carolrhoda Books
A division of Lerner Publishing Group, Inc.
241 First Avenue North
Minneapolis, MN 55401 USA

For reading levels and more information, look up this title at www.lernerbooks.com.

Cover background: © iStockphoto.com/manley099.

Main body text set in LumarcLL 14/20. Typeface provided by Linotype.

Library of Congress Cataloging-in-Publication Data

Friedman, Laurie B., 1964-
    Game Time, Mallory! / by Laurie Friedman ; illustrations by Jennifer Kalis.
        pages cm. — (Mallory ; #23)
    Summary: Mallory is excited to participate in a new girls' basketball
league, although she has never played and her best friends are not
interested, but as the worst player on her team she realizes she has a lot
to learn.
    ISBN 978-1-4677-0923-1 (trade hard cover : alk. paper)
    ISBN 978-1-4677-6188-8 (EB pdf)
    [1. Basketball—Fiction. 2. Self-confidence—Fiction. 3. Teamwork (Sports)—
ction. 4. Friendship—Fiction.] I. Kalis, Jennifer, illustrator. II. Title.
    .F89773Wro 2015
    —dc23   2014001769

red in the United States of America
/31/15